W9-BHE-357

After the Rain

by Rebecca Koehn

illustrated by Simone Krüger

beaming books

MINNEAPOLIS

Text copyright © 2020 Rebecca Koehn
Illustrations copyright © 2020 Beaming Books

Published in 2020 by Beaming Books,
an imprint of 1517 Media. All rights reserved.
No part of this book may be reproduced
without the written permission of the publisher.
Email copyright@1517.media.
Printed in the United States of America.

26 25 24 23 22 21 20   1 2 3 4 5 6 7 8

ISBN: 9781506454511

Library of Congress Cataloging-in-Publication Data
Names: Koehn, Rebecca, author. | Kruger, Simone, illustrator.
Title: After the rain / by Rebecca Koehn ; illustrated by Simone Krüger.
Description: Minneapolis, MN : Beaming Books, 2020. | Audience: Ages 5-8. |
    Summary: When a stream of rainwater carries Levi's boat to where Polly
    is playing, she starts a puddle fight but as the water begins to
    disappear, they must work together to prolong their fun.
Identifiers: LCCN 2019034488 | ISBN 9781506454511 (hardcover)
Subjects: CYAC: Play--Fiction. | Puddles--Fiction. | Rain and
    rainfall--Fiction.
Classification: LCC PZ7.1.K6733 Aft 2020 | DDC [E]--dc23
LC record available at https://lccn.loc.gov/2019034488

Beaming Books
510 Marquette Avenue
Minneapolis, MN 55402
Beamingbooks.com

VN0004589; 9781506454511; JAN2020

Drip.

Drop.

Plink.

The rain is over.

The gutter
overflows.

Levi grabs
his boat.

Water rushes,
 roils,
  ripples.

The boat floats.

Levi runs ahead.

A river rages,
plunges, lunges.

Swirling twigs. Whirling leaves.

The boat
races!

Uh oh! Polly!

"My river. No boats here!"
Polly says.

Hmm. Levi dodges.

Polly stomps!

A battle begins.

The
battle
rages.

But then—no splash.
Just a splish.

No roiling.
No rippling.
Instead, tinkling and dribbling.

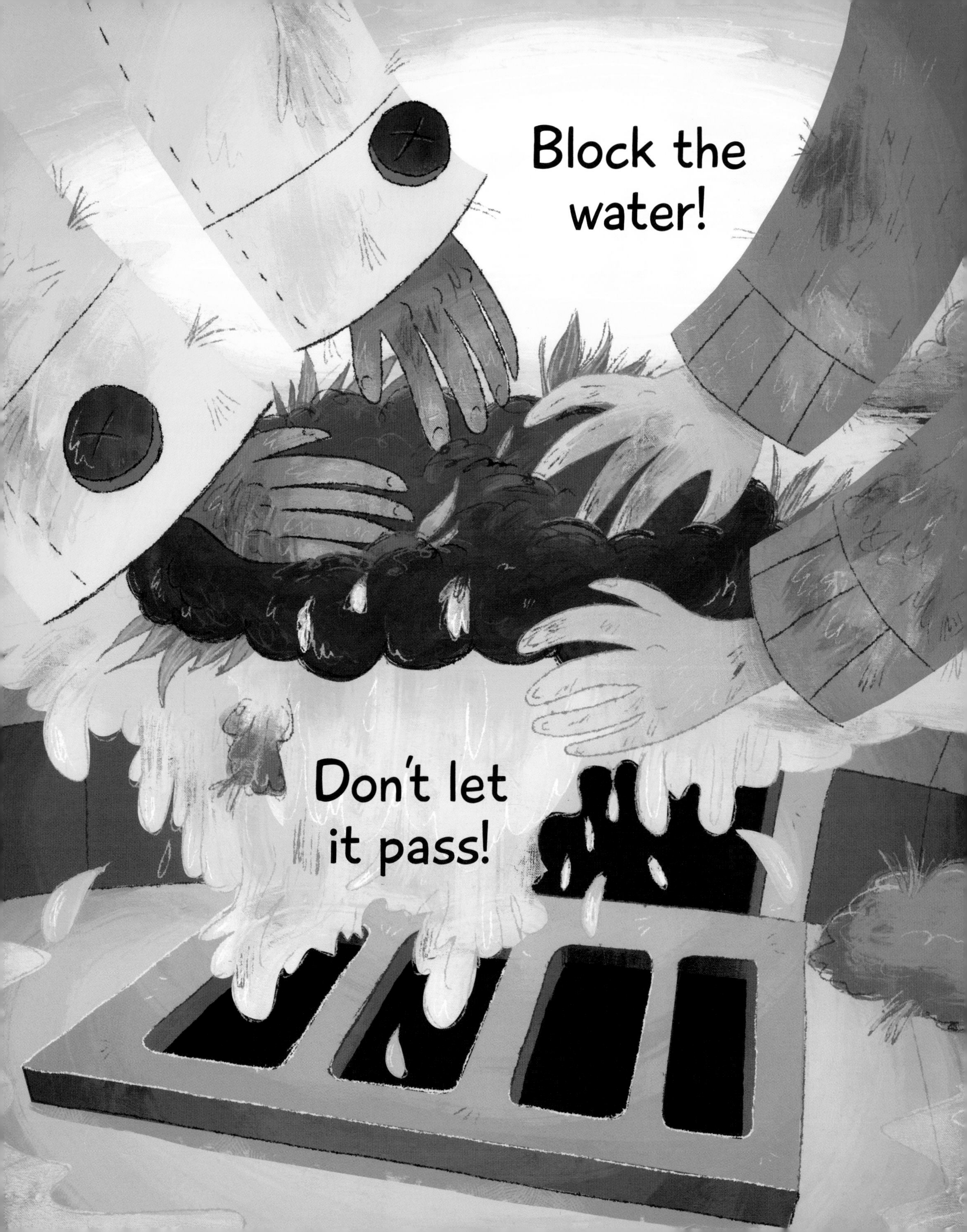
Block the water!
Don't let it pass!

Build a dam!

Hurry! It's going!

Shaping dirt!

Piling rocks.

Stuffing leaves.

Stacking sticks.

The water stops.

No more river.

A lake.

Polly constructs.

Levi shapes.

A town
grows from
mud and muck.

Battle begun
but not won.

Building together is
much more fun!

About the Author and Illustrator

REBECCA KOEHN is a teacher and children's book author who lives on the windy Kansas prairie. She enjoys playing in puddles after a rain, walking her Husky, Hazel, and playing board games with her husband and sons.

SIMONE KRÜGER is a Germany-based children's book illustrator. She loves being out and about in the countryside, discovering nature and new creatures to draw. When it starts to rain, you can see her wearing a bright yellow raincoat. As a kid, she loved playing barefoot in the rain and splashing in puddles.